The Curate's Brother:

A Jane Austen Variation of Persuasion

a short story

Wendy Van Camp

This book is a work of fiction. Names, characters, places, and incidents are products of the author's imagination or are used fictionally. Any resemblance to actual persons, events, or locales is entirely coincidental.

Cover by Wendy Van Camp

The Curate's Brother: A Jane Austen Variation of Persuasion

Copyright © 2015 Wendy Van Camp

ISBN-10: 1507763980
ISBN-13: 978-1507763988

DEDICATION

To my husband.

Thank you for all your love and support.

THE CURATE'S BROTHER

1806 – MONKFORD
SOMERSETSHIRE, ENGLAND

Edward Wentworth, the curate of Monkford, in Somersetshire, was on his knees in his garden. He was not in prayer, but in the task of pulling weeds from the herbal patch that grew near the kitchen door of his cottage. Summer was approaching and the plants had thrived in the rich soil and temperate climate.

As he yanked on a stubborn weed, he heard the crunch of boots on the gravel path near the garden's gate and then a hearty laugh. At the gate stood a broad shouldered man in a blue and gold naval uniform. The man tucked a bicorn hat under his arm. "That is quite the battle. Who will win, the man or the weed?"

"I beg your pardon?" Edward stood and dusted the earth from his trousers. Who the devil was this? He looked the sailor over. The man wore his black hair tied back with a ribbon, a face that had seen more sun than not, and blue eyes that reminded him of his mother's. The years transposed in his mind and he could see the vestiges of the twelve year old boy that had left his father's home for the sea. "Frederick? Could it be you?"

"I see that I have outpaced my letter." Opening the white washed gate, his brother stepped into the garden. "It is good to see you, Edward. It's been a period."

Edward clasped his brother in a warm embrace. It had been well over seven years since he had last seen his elder brother. Frederick had been on station in the West Indies since he was a midshipman and seldom came back to England.

"When did you return? Last you wrote, you were in some sort of action. San Domingo was it?"

Frederick nodded at the name and a fleeting look crossed his expression. "Under orders, I sailed a prize frigate back to Plymouth. It was my first command." The good natured countenance returned. "We arrived last week. Once I secured the ship, they released me on leave."

Edward gestured toward the kitchen door and the two brothers entered the cottage. They walked through the kitchen and down the hall until they reached his study. A pair of wingback chairs faced the hearth and walls lined with books. A small credenza held a tray with a couple of letters upon it, all laid in a precise stack. Edward rang for tea and then changed his mind. He had spirits tucked away for special occasions.

Lifting a glass bottle from a cabinet in the credenza he asked, "Brandy?"

"Aye. That would be most welcome." Frederick settled into a leather wingback chair. Edward poured two glasses and handed one to his brother. His brother lifted the glass. "To the King." Edward lifted his glass and echoed his brother.

"Where are you bags? You didn't walk all the way here from Monkford?"

"I gained your direction from the innkeeper and managed to catch a ride on a wagon most of the way. It felt good to stretch my legs in the exploration of a new land." Frederick cast his attention around the room. "You have a comfortable situation here, Brother. Imagine, all this space for a single soul?"

"Quite. I have all the space I need for study or to tend to my duties. It is ideal."

"I've never had more than a cabin the length of my bed to call my own, but to compensate, I've seen much of the world." Frederick looked about the room. "The quiet here is remarkable, hardly a whisper around us. On the ship, you are aware of all the souls aboard."

"Rather like my flock."

Frederick gave a hearty laugh. "We press the hands from the prisons of England. They take a steady eye and a quick whip to keep in line until you gain their respect." He took a drink from his glass. "Not quite the same."

Was Frederick mocking him? He studied his

brother. No, it was not that. Edward suspected that the war had touched his brother in a manner that would not show on the surface. He re-answered his brother's question. "It is true that I live alone, save for my housekeeper. For the length of your leave, I could share. There is a spare room upstairs. We'll have Mr. Jenkins send your trunk in the morning."

Frederick lifted his glass in a toast. "I did not want to ask, but if you are offering."

"How could I not? It is not every day your brother comes home from the sea." Edward gave his brother a reassuring look and Frederick's posture relaxed. "Welcome home, brother."

###

Stepping out into the soft morning sunshine the following Sunday, Edward found his accustomed place to one side of the doorway of the Monkford church. His Vicar took the other. A mother and father followed by four children were the first to depart. The father stopping to chat with the Vicar before the family set off to walk home. This was his first day at church since his brother arrived. That Frederick wanted to come to service and see what he did for his living, pleased Edward.

"Good day, Mr. Wentworth." The voice was soft, feminine and familiar.

"Thank you for the biscuits, Miss Marshall. It was kind of you to bring them to the cottage."

The girl blushed, the ringlets of her hair giving a pleasant bounce as she dipped her head. Was this the young girl that brought biscuits to his doorstep or help organize the contents of the poor box after services? That memory did not fit the girl standing before him now, wearing an adult frock and a bonnet to protect her complexion. He found the juxtaposition of Sally the child and the adult clothing of the newly come out Miss Marshall to be disconcerting.

Miss Marshall's attention shifted and her eyes grew wide. Edward noticed his brother, wearing ill-fitting cast offs from the church in place of his naval uniform, had come to join him. He was giving Miss Marshall a casual grin that warred with his feral appraisal that swept over her form. The girl's eyelashes fluttered and she blushed. Edward felt a wave of discomfort start in his gut and flow to his chest.

"Would you do the honor of introducing me to your fair companion?"

Miss Marshall looked at Edward with expectation and a flash of excitement. He prevented himself from grimacing. "Miss Sally Marshall, may I introduce my brother, Commander Frederick Wentworth of his Majesty's Royal Navy. Frederick, this is Miss Marshall, the daughter of the village apothecary." Sally gave a polite curtsy to his brother's bow and the introduction became complete.

More families streamed through the open double doors of the church, filling the narrow porch. Sally dimpled and said, "Welcome to Monkford, Commander. Will you be staying long with us?'

"As long as the admiralty allows, Miss Marshall. I am awaiting reassignment."

Miss Marshall's smile diminished, but she rallied. "Mr. Wentworth, you simply must bring your brother to the assembly next week."

"You have not mentioned an assembly, Edward." There was a good natured prodding in Frederick's voice.

He faced his brother. "I am sure that I would have in time." Turning back to Sally, "We will both attend, Miss Marshall, you can be certain."

The girl gave a clap of her gloved hands and this time her winsome smile included both men. "What delightful news. I look forward to telling Papa." More people were crowding the narrow entry. The girl gave a quick curtsy to the brothers and continued down the steps where her family was waiting.

"What an amiable girl. You have been holding out on me, Edward. I wonder what other delights Monkford will hold."

"Frederick, Miss Marshall is a respectable girl and the daughter of a friend. If you intend to ruin this girl's reputation…" A hand from his seafaring brother on his shoulder stopped him.

"I am returning to sea soon enough. I have no intention of starting a complication here. Come, greet your parish. Say no more." Edward studied his brother's face and saw no guile there. He relaxed. One after another, the people exited the church, pausing either with himself or with the Vicar across the way.

There did not seem to be a preference by the people of Monkford between the elder Vicar and the Curate. Though Edward was a scant two and twenty years of age, he was as respected as the Vicar. At least, until the baronet's family from Kellynch Hall exited the church.

Sir Walter Elliot wore a puce frock coat and appeared well groomed, to the point that his coiffure would be the envy of women. His silver headed cane gleamed in the morning light. An elegant woman of similar age followed along with two young women. The first girl had elaborate braids, perfect skin, and a dress of the finest cut and quality. The other was pale, exhibiting fragility. She wore the sprig muslin of an innocent. Sir Walter never stopped to speak to Edward, a mere curate. He would only acknowledge the Vicar when he and his family came to church.

He heard a catch of breath behind him. "Who is that beautiful creature, Edward?"

Edward glanced back to learn who his brother was speaking of and realized he was looking at the baronet's daughters. "Miss Elliot is the belle of Somersetshire. She is Sir Walter Elliot's eldest daughter. Reputed to be the heiress of quite a fortune." There was much speculation about whom Miss Elliot would settle on. Perhaps a man of wealth and title would be able to tempt the golden haired beauty. Sir Walter was in excellent health and while Miss Elliot was quite eligible, neither father nor daughter was in a hurry to find a match.

"No, no, not the fancy one. The one behind her with the brown hair, the lady's companion? Pretty little thing she is."

"That is no companion. Miss Anne Elliot is Sir Walter's second daughter."

"She is like a pocket sprite, you could just scoop her up and put her in your…"

"Frederick, please. There are people about."

Across the way, Anne Elliot had noticed his brother's regard. Her pale face colored a becoming pink and she looked away.

"Such a shy one. It might be fun to draw her out."

"Frederick, did you not pay heed? She is the daughter of a baronet. Come to your senses man." While their father had been wealthy enough to buy Frederick's commission in the navy and to sponsor Edward an education at Cambridge, they were of the merchant class, no match in status for someone of the peerage.

His brother followed the girl's progress down the steps as Sir Walter led his party to the carriage that waited at the end of the lane. "Brother, you will learn that sometimes risk has its reward." Anne Elliot entered the carriage and a footman closed the door. His brother turned from the girl and gave Edward his full attention. "Why are you convinced that I have come to cause your doom? Do you think so little of me?"

Edward deflated. "No. I suppose I keep thinking of you as the twelve year old scamp that insisted he was for the sea until father gave in to your desires. I do not know the man that has come back to England. At least, not yet."

"Fair enough. We need a shakedown cruise to clear the decks between us." Frederick moved behind Edward to allow more of the parishioners to exit the church. "I hope that we both prove to each other's satisfaction."

###

The next day, the two brothers were loading Edward's small farmer's cart in front of the church. Frederick arranged blankets, cast off clothing and baskets of food in the small pallet area behind the driver's bench. His brother's skilled hands tied down the offerings with a rope. The sailor looked up at the sun and then addressed his brother. "We are high into morning. Should we not be off?"

"Soon." Edward stroked the nose of his old gelding, feeling the horse' breath on his fingers. He reached into his pocket and pulled out a small carrot and held it out on his flat palm. The animal crunched the vegetable in its strong teeth. Blast. Where was the girl?

There was a flash of blonde hair peeking over the stone fence that led off from the church yard. Sally Marshall opened the wooden gate and came into view. Dressed as if on a Sunday outing, she had a large basket perched on her arm. "Good day, Mr. Wentworth. I hope the morning finds you well?" She gave Edward a polite curtsy, more of a bounce than a formal ritual greeting.

"I am well, but I had all but thought your father had changed his mind about the medicine."

"Oh no, Mr. Wentworth. Papa would never do that to Mother Higgins." She gestured to the basket. "I made her a pomade myself." She held up an orange studded with cloves. "My father sent a tincture that he believes will ease her pain."

Frederick held out his hand. "Might I relieve your burden, Miss Marshall?"

The girl startled at the sound of his brother's voice. She allowed his brother to take the basket and add it to the others. Sally watched the sailor's movements as he shifted the load. Frederick finished his task and turned back, which caused Sally to spin to Edward. "Her daughter does not think she will last beyond the summer, Mr. Wentworth." The words were calm and steady, warring with the spring of her curls.

"Indeed. I will visit her family later this afternoon and pray with her." He would pass on Mother Higgins' condition to the Vicar and do what he could to ease her last months on this Earth. Miss Marshall was young; Edward did not wish to burden the child with ill news.

"Is there anything more that I could do?"

"No child. Go with God and give my thanks to your father." Miss Marshall fell silent and seemed to withdraw. Edward felt confused by her reaction. Had he not thanked the girl properly? Why such disappointment?

Edward swung up into the driver's seat and picked up the reins. Frederick joined him on the bench. With a slap of the reins on the gelding's rump, the rickety cart set off down the road and left Miss Marshall standing alone in the yard.

As the sun reached its zenith, Frederick removed his borrowed coat and draped it over the side rail. He loosened his caveat and leaned back, his boots perched against a foot rest. Edward did not feel comfortable doing the same, although the summer sun created a trickle of sweat down his back. He would present a respectable appearance as they traveled, one worthy of his profession.

"How often do you go out to the parish?"

Frederick swatted at a blowfly that buzzed around his head.

"Three times a week. This is why the Vicar accepted me as his assistant. I do the physical aspects of tending the flock so the Vicar can focus on the sermons and the gentry."

"He is too good to get his hands dirty?"

Edward chuckled. "Do you do the tasks of the lowest deckhand on your ship?"

"Every young gentleman learns to climb the masts, tie knots and other duties. Our training is not all letters and navigation. Once we become officers, we are as skilled as the hands. How else are we to train the men?"

"Most Vicars and Rectors start as a curate like myself. We learn to tend our flocks before taking on a full living. We are not so different, Brother."

Frederick leaned back in the seat, ignoring the bumps and rattles of the road. "Perhaps, but I confess that I could never stay in one small village for my entire life. Not when there was an entire world to explore."

###

Pulling up to the humble cottage of the Higgins family, Edward tied the reins to a rail of the cart before he jumped from the bench. He took the bridle of his horse and stood while he waited for the farmer.

"Mr. Wentworth!" Higgins strode from the shed to one side. "Let me take that fine horse of yours. Herself has been waiting for your arrival all morning."

Frederick had gone to the cart and removed a large basket from the back, before joining Edward. As the farmer took the gelding, the two brothers walked to the door of the cottage.

Mrs. Higgins was a worn woman with five children and a sick mother-in-law that needed constant tending. Her relief at the sight of Edward and his brother was evident. She took the basket from Frederick even as Edward finished introducing his brother. When he mentioned that his brother was an officer in the navy, the woman paused in her inventory of the basket of food and medicines.

"Mary? Perhaps you could give Commander Wentworth a tour of the farm?" She smiled at Frederick with the predatory gleam of a woman with an unmarried daughter. "I'm sure that my daughter will make your stay with us more pleasant, sir."

Frederick gave his brother a helpless look as the

young woman sauntered to him. She dipped a curtsy. Frederick returned a polite bow, even as Edward gave him a warning shake of his head. Edward said nothing as his brother joined Mary. With his brother gone, there was more space inside the small cottage, allowing Mrs. Higgins room to unpack the basket of food.

Edward settled into a wooden chair at the elderly woman's beside. Mrs. Higgins prepared the tincture that the apothecary sent in the basket while they chatted with the elderly woman. Mrs. Higgins served the tea, the tincture to Mother Higgins and an Earl Grey to himself. Edward opened his bible and the three discussed scripture until Mother Higgins fell asleep.

Edward stood and took Mrs. Higgins aside where their conversation would not wake the elderly woman. "There has been no improvement in your Mother-in-law?"

"None, Mr. Wentworth. She is fading from this world."

"The tincture will ease her pain until she is called to God. I will return soon. If you need anything, send one of your children to the church."

"I will, Mr. Wentworth. Thank you for your kindness."

"It is the least I can do, Mrs. Higgins."

They stepped outside the cottage where Mr. Higgins was parading his best cow in front of Frederick and his daughter. His brother was doing his best to be polite, but the relief on his face was plain when Edward came to join him. After they called their farewells to Mr. Higgins and his disappointed daughter, Edward had reins in hand and his brother on the seat beside him.

"He invited us to dinner. I was not sure if I could

accept without your consent."

"Did you want to attend?"

"Uh...I would rather not. Why on god's earth was that man showing his cattle to me? I could not understand half of what he was talking about."

"He was not showing you a cow, Frederick. He was showing you his wealth and how suitable his daughter's dowry is should you care for a match."

"What?" Frederick turned on the bench to look back at the farm with a puzzled expression.

"With the war draining so many men from England, any eligible bachelor with an income is a draw. Your officer's half-pay would go far toward the support of a farmer's daughter."

Frederick shuddered. "If I marry, it will be to a lady mild of manner, steady of character and some education. Mary Higgins should seek elsewhere."

Edward grinned. "I concur, Brother. We are both far too young to consider settling down."

"Aye." Frederick leaned back on the bench to be more comfortable on the bumpy road.

###

The Wentworth brothers arrived at the public assembly the following week. Edward handed his gelding to the groom and caught his brother straightening the ill-fitting dark coat he had borrowed from him.

"Nervous?" Edward said as the pair walked toward the large brick building. The sound of music wafted on the wind and the scent of citrus and cinnamon tickled their nostrils.

"Before a battle I feel sourness in my belly. The heft of my hanger seems to steady me."

"Leave your sword home; I doubt you'll need it with the ladies, except to fend them off. I have it on good report that you've caused quite a stir among them." Gossip traveled with speed when there was someone new in the parish. His housekeeper had let Edward know that the tongues of Monkford were wagging about the young naval commander. The attention his brother garnered amused him, but he also felt a sense of family pride. Frederick was moving up in the world and was a credit to them all.

Frederick snorted. "It is not me, it's the uniform." As they walked along the path to the assembly hall entrance, his brother said, "Still, I suppose the thrill of the chase remains. Who knows what we will find this evening?"

Inside the assembly hall, the people of Monkford gathered. Bright light from windows filled the large hall. A quintet warmed up their strings with the sweet treble of violins and the warmer tones of cello.

At the door, their host greeted them. "I say, welcome Mr. Wentworth and you as well, Commander. What a thrill it is to have the hero of San Domingo here in our little village."

Frederick glanced at Edward in surprise, "Hero?" he mouthed to his brother. Edward nodded in confirmation. While news from London was slow, the news of Frederick's heroism and the commendation awarded him by Admiral Duckworth was making the circles in Monkford.

"Oh come now, it was all written in the Navy Gazette. I must say, the story of how you saved your ship and took that frigate is inspiring. You will need to relay all the details tonight over port."

Frederick shifted from one foot to another and

pulled on his cravat. "It would be my honor to tell you more this evening, Sir Henry. However, I was hoping to stand up with a few of the ladies first."

Sir Henry laughed. "I understand, Commander. Go and make merry."

The two men left the knight behind and winnowed their way through the throng of people that pressed into the foyer. "You will need to prepare yourself, brother. I doubt that will be the last request." Edward sidestepped a pair of ladies in pale gowns with glittering combs in their hair. "The headline in the Gazette was quite provocative."

It was astonishing to see his brother's normal exuberance change into a somber expression. "I would rather not. I was no hero. I did what the ship needed to survive." Edward wondered, not for the first time, what dangers his brother faced in the West Indies. Perhaps that explained his need to throw himself into the society here in Somerset.

The pair entered the main room where the musicians were preparing the evening's entertainment. A host of young men and women were milling about, waiting for the dances to begin. There was a flash of bobbing curls and young Sally ducked into view, dressed in a becoming confection of peach and cream. There was a new quality about her, something that he could not quite put his finger on. Instead of joining Edward, she rushed to his brother. "Commander, how splendid it is that you have come."

Frederick's expression shifted into a twinkle of gaiety as he bent a short bow. "I am delighted to have pleased you, Miss Marshall. Might I inquire if you have room on your dance card for a wayward sailor?"

Sally giggled. "Of course, Sir."

"Then might I claim the next two dances?"

Edward watched the conversation with some surprise. A muscle in his cheek twitched.

Sally blushed, her curls bobbing among its ribbons. She handed him her card and the pencil tied to it. Frederick wrote his name into the first two slots. "There, it is done. I will collect you shortly, my dear."

Without a glance at Edward, Sally flashed his brother a smile and disappeared into the crowd. No doubt to crow over her acquisition of "the hero of San Domingo".

"Was that necessary?" Edward could not disguise the irritation in his voice.

Frederick's eyes widened. "All I did was ask the girl to dance. She seems a pretty thing. Why should I not?" He then looked contrite. "Edward, I am sorry. I had not realized that you and…"

"There is nothing to realize." Edward was curt, but he felt confused about why. He admitted that he had grown fond of the child, but it could be no more than that. Sally Marshall was free to dance with whomever she wished.

"I am glad that we have cleared that up." The opening strains of the musicians began. He gave Edward a nod and then set sail in search of his dance partner. Edward found his way to the punch bowl and helped himself to a glass.

At a fashionably late hour, the quintet paused mid-song. The dancers halted in their reel and all heads turned to the entrance of the assembly hall. There stood Sir Walter Elliot, resplendent in his bright celadon coat and starched lace ruffles. He surveyed the hall with a sniff before coming to meet the host.

"Good day to you, Sir Walter." His hurried exertion across the hall had turned the elderly knight's face red. "You and your family are most welcome here, Sir."

"Quite." Sir Walter waited as his family entered the hall. His eldest daughter, Elizabeth took to her father's arm. Edward knew that the young woman played the hostess for her father and managed the house with the finesse of her departed mother, the former Lady Elliot. On Sir Walter's other side, the elegant Lady Russell stood, of advanced years but still strong and in her full faculties. Edward stayed clear of the lady, because his Vicar had warned him to be cautious near her. Last to arrive was Sir Elliot's second daughter, Anne. She seemed to melt into the shadows despite all the attention her family garnered.

"May I present my daughter Miss Elliot?" The elegant blonde curtsied to Sir Henry. "You will remember, Lady Russell." The matron gave a nod of her head to the knight, the plume on her turban dancing in the air.

The knight seemed to expect a third introduction, but the baronet fell silent.

"Er…do be welcome, Sir Walter." Sir Henry turned and motioned to the quintet and the music filled the assembly hall. Within moments the men and women resumed their reel. Sir Walter made his way to the card room, leaving his daughters and the matron behind.

As a group of young men surrounded the coy Miss Elliot, who poked at them with her fan and laughed at their jokes. Edward noticed that Miss Anne made her way to the side of the room where the wallflowers found their chairs. He had heard little of the younger Elliot daughter, except that she was prone to walking and reading books. There was a shuffle of boots and Edward noted that Frederick returned from the dance floor. Thus far, the sailor had not missed a single reel and to Edward's growing ire, had danced with young Sally more than twice this evening. It was quite improper of him, but no one else seemed to mind. Not yet.

"I can not decide if an admiral has piped aboard or if a peacock has spread its tail in full display. The man even checked his hair in the mirror before he entered the card room."

"Sir Walter is somewhat…eccentric."

"That is one way of putting it." Frederick jabbed him in the ribs. "With the father away, now would be a good time for you to introduce me to his daughter."

Edward grimaced. Did his brother not comprehend his position in the shire? There could be nothing good of his pursuing an Elliot. "Are you sure you want to take your place in her court? With beauty and that dowry, you may find yourself dueling at dawn with one of her suitors."

Frederick snorted, "Not that one. The sister. See, she is there unattended at the wall."

Edward followed his brother's direction where the quiet Miss Anne sat alone. She was not unchaperoned, for Lady Russell was chatting nearby with a few of the older women. He gave his brother a speculative glance. If Frederick was busy with the Elliot daughter, perhaps he would stay away from Sally.

"Very well." Edward made his way around the perimeter of the room until he stood before the baronet's daughter. She looked up from her chair in astonishment and rose to her feet. "Good day, Miss Anne. I hope I find you well this evening."

"I am quite well, Mr. Wentworth." She shifted her attention between Edward and his brother who had followed behind him.

"May I present to you, Commander Frederick

Wentworth. Frederick, this is Miss Anne Elliot."

The girl dipped a curtsy as Frederick bowed in return. "I was wondering if you might do me the honor of your first two dances, Miss Anne."

The girl paled and opened her mouth, but no words issued forth. Edward knew her sister tended to dominate any room the pair was in. The girl was not familiar to male attention. "Go on, Miss Anne. Take a chance." Edward surprised himself with the sympathy he felt for the shy girl. "My brother is well behaved," he paused and said, "Well, most of the time."

Frederick held out his hand to the girl and offered a steady gaze into her brown eyes. "Stand up with me, Miss Anne. The music is about to begin." His seafaring brother wiggled his brows and half his mouth pulled into a grin.

Mesmerized by his expression, Anne asked, "Are

you fond of music, Commander?"

Frederick's mouth shifted into a full smile. "I am when it includes dancing with a pretty partner." A blush bloomed on Miss Anne's cheeks and her eyes widened. Miss Anne inched her hand forward until it slipped into Frederick's palm. He closed his hand around hers.

The pair made their way onto the dance floor. Edward watched them before he retreated to the window at the far side of the hall. How curious that his brother would choose a wallflower when so many of the ladies were seeking his company.

The music and laughter of the assembly retreated as Edward examined his reflection in the window pane. His pronounced nose and dark eyes, features that he shared with their sister Sophia, did not stir the ladies the way that his brother's carefree countenance did. Edward was careful with his life; a curate had to or else face an uncertain future without a home or profession. He had known this when he had took his orders, but until now it had not weighed on him as it did this night.

Until his brother's arrival, he had lived a quiet life in his shabby cottage, content with his lot. He planted his garden in straight rows and followed a schedule to visit the people of Monkford in even rotation. He was a man of two and twenty, on the first rung of the ladder of his profession. All Edward owned was the clothes on his back, the books in his library, and a small savings invested in the percents.

With his brother now occupied with another, Edward wondered who was dancing with Sally. He had always thought of her as a child; a ragamuffin with smudges on her cheeks, running errands for her father. Tonight, there was a difference in her. Sally had come out this past spring, as most girls of seventeen did, dressed as a lady and garnering attention as a woman. Her youth and innocence had not prevented Frederick from action tonight. He had asked for his dances and found reward with smiles and acceptance. What did Edward gain with his slow and respectable manner? Ignored.

Edward turned back to the assembly where the couples danced in long lines, weaving in their prescribed patterns. Was he old before his time? To stand against the wall alone while his heroic brother danced with all the pretty women and made merry? Edward shuffled his feet and clasped his hands behind his back. Most rectors and vicars did marry after all; they made enough of a living to support a wife and children. It was logical to suppose that before one married, one had to court a woman. Perhaps a mere curate did not make enough, but would he remain a curate all his life?

Across the room, Edward's attention fell upon Sally Marshall. She was laughing with one of the Poole brothers while a widowed farmer, a man in his thirties with four children, stood beside her enraptured. Edward was not pleased to see John Poole with Sally, but at least he was within girl's tender age. The widower was another matter. It was time that Edward follow his brother's example. He would take a risk and rescue Sally from the widower.

"Mr. Wentworth, might I have a word with you?" From the crowd, a green turban with a bobbing purple feather appeared before him, interrupting his thoughts. Edward performed a respectful bow to Lady Russell. The widow had spoken to him on two previous occasions and that because formality had forced her. He recollected his Vicar's warning about the old harridan.

"Of course. I am at your service."

"I am wondering, who is that man you introduced to my god-daughter? I do not recall seeing him before."

"He is my elder brother, Frederick Wentworth of the Royal Navy. He noticed that Miss Anne had not been asked to dance and thought that he would be of service."

"I see." The woman lifted her lorgnette to peer at Anne and Frederick as they stood opposite each other in a reel. The girl was gaining a bloom on her cheeks that brought life to her pale face. Edward could not decide if it was from the movement of the dance or the way his brother was gazing into her eyes every time the dance brought them closer together.

"It is a public assembly, Lady Russell. What harm is it for the girl to join in with the other young women?"

"She is not just another young woman," the matron informed him. "She is my god-daughter. I promised on her mother's death-bed that I would look after her." The lorgnette popped down and she bore her stare upon Edward. "I will allow it tonight out of honor for Sir Henry, but no further familiarity. My Anne will have a good match with a man of title, not some sailor fresh off the docks."

Edward bristled. As annoyed as he was with Frederick paying court to Sally, this insult touched on their family's honor. "I assure you, your god-daughter is safe," he gestured to the hall at large, "in this most public of assemblies." Edward produced a shallow bow. "Good day to you, Madam." He stalked off before he said something he would regret.

As he marched the perimeter of the hall, Edward reminded himself that Lady Russell had great influence with the upper circles of Somersetshire. He may have blundered being curt with her.

Sally was still with the widower and Mr. Poole as they waited for the next dance to begin. Edward continued his progress toward her. For a moment, he shared a look with Sally. Edward felt his heart beat in anticipation of their meeting. Then the girl turned and leaned against Mr. Poole's offered arm. They exchanged a few words and the man led her out to the dance floor. Edward halted. There was no need of him to rescue the girl from the widower after all. Mr. Poole had taken that duty from him.

Edward retreated into the back room where the men smoked cigars and played cards. While he did not join in the games, he found comfort in their jovial banter and in conversation of the church. It was his own comfortable world and where he belonged. Here he was able to pass the rest of the evening without dealing with women, either young or old.

###

A few days after the assembly, the two brothers were once again sharing Edward's parish rounds. There was little conversation between them. Each brother lost in his own thoughts. The clatter of the gelding's hooves made a cadence on the hard packed earth as they traveled.

Edward had put the dance and Sally's manner behind him. He had duties to perform for his parish and could not afford to waste his time on a flirtatious schoolgirl. Frederick struck him as bored, even so, he had been willing to come. Perhaps the road was less boring than remaining in the cottage all day.

Edward drove into the main yard of a prosperous farm and a groom came from the stable to take the bridle of his horse. The young curate gave the man a nod of recognition as he left the cart. This time there was no basket of food for the poor. The Bowers had no need, but Edward would not neglect their spiritual needs.

Upon his knock, a servant in a starched white apron and grey attire opened the door. "Good day to you, Mr. Wentworth. Are you here to see Madam Bower?"

"I am indeed. Is she receiving visitors?"

"She always looks forward to your visit, Mr. Wentworth. Although, I will say, you are not the first to arrive. Please follow me."

The servant led the pair to the rear of the house. A couch placed where its occupant could have a view of the countryside through a wide window. Seated beside the elderly woman was Anne Elliot, dressed in a colorful blue frock that enhanced her delicate features. The girl held an open book in her lap. As Edward and his brother entered, she stood and gave the brothers a curtsy.

"Good day to you, Miss Anne. I believe that you remember my brother?"

"I do, Mr. Wentworth." Anne's complexion seemed brighter and the smile she displayed to his brother was radiant. The transformation from pale wallflower was quite remarkable.

Edward intended to say more, but discovered his brother standing still as a bronze statue, staring at Anne Elliot. Frederick's mouth was open as if he had intended to speak, but not a sound issued forth.

The girl tilted her head to one side and gave a half smile. A hand covered her mouth as if she were afraid to show her merriment. At last, Frederick managed to find his tongue. "What are you reading, Miss Elliot?" He gestured to the book tucked under her arm.

"A selection of William Cowper to Mrs. Bower." Still looking at his brother she recited from memory. "Existence is a strange bargain. Life owes us little; we owe it everything…"

Frederick startled at her words and broke in, "The only true happiness comes from squandering ourselves for a purpose." Edward stared in silent astonishment, since when did his brother read literature?

Miss Anne relaxed and looked at his brother with favor. "You have read William Cowper? He is one of my favorite authors."

"My former Captain had one of Cowper's books in his personal library. We read it as part of learning our letters as midshipmen." Frederick's stance relaxed as well.

Mrs. Bower touched Anne's hand. "My dear, now that the curate is here, perhaps you could take a turn around the gardens for an hour or so. This young officer would be happy to escort you, I'm certain."

"It would be my pleasure, Miss Anne. Perhaps we could discuss more of Cowper as we stroll." He offered his arm and the girl placed her hand on it. Her steps were light on the floor, soundless as if her feet did not touch the earth. The pair exited through the French doors at the rear of the room and was soon lost among the roses outside.

"You are kind to my brother, Mrs. Bower." Edward said as he took the chair that Anne had vacated. "I've never seen him so distracted."

"Nor have I seen Anne as taken with a gentleman. Your brother is a handsome young man. According to the gossip, he was quite the hero in the West Indies and thus has prospects." The matron smiled. "I detect quite an air of the Irish in him."

"Our mother was from the emerald isle. Frederick favors her more than our sister and I. How are you feeling? You seem much improved from my last visit."

"Anne has been coming to read to me. I confess that it lifts this old woman's spirits to have such a cultured companion. I had wondered at her new bloom. Now I believe I know the cause of it."

Edward agreed with the matron. Miss Anne was no longer a pale wraith hiding in the shadows, but seemed quite engaged with her surroundings. Quiet and demure, she portrayed a type of woman that most Englishmen would find attractive, including his brother. "But she is a baronet's daughter. Sir Walter will never approve."

"Pish posh. Sir Walter only cares about Elizabeth. She is the one required to marry a man with a title. The younger Elliot might make a choice more to her liking."

"Mrs. Bower, are you proposing something?"

"While it is true I will be free from my couch soon. No one need know. I will continue to ask for Anne to visit me as a lady's companion. Her father and godmother will not deny me such a small pleasure. At the same time, if the Commander pleases, he is welcome to visit our estate. I will be their chaperon so no impropriety will occur. Let Cupid's arrow fall where it may."

Edward opened his missal to the passage he was

planning on discussion with Mrs. Bower that day. "I will bring up the idea to him, Mrs. Bower, but I fear that little good will come from this."

"Then it is well that others are here to do god's will. Now, Mr. Wentworth, I believe that we were to talk about more of god's work?"

Edward bent his head and began to read from the missal.

###

Edward entered the kitchen and meandered to the sideboard where Mrs. Bates had placed the day's breakfast items. There was porridge, eggs shirred with milk and a selection of sliced ham. Mrs. Bates poured Edward a cup of tea using the willow china that had belonged to his mother. Edward noticed that the plate of biscuits that accompanied the tea was absent. In fact, he realized they had been missing for quite some time.

As Edward settled into his accustomed place at

table, his brother strode into the room. There was much clanking of platters as Frederick heaped his plate and then joined him at the opposite end. His brother was well groomed with a fresh ribbon tying back his black hair. As Frederick speared a slice of ham, he mumbled, "Morning."

Edward snorted into his tea. Two days ago, Frederick had gone to the tailor and fitted for new clothing. He declared himself done with wearing cast-offs and wanted a coat that fit his frame and made him more presentable in society.

"Back to the Bower's?" Edward asked. It would be the third time this week.

Frederick set down his fork with feigned dignity. "If you must know, yes I am. I need to borrow the gelding." Edward frowned. He had scheduled a trip to the Higgins Farm this afternoon to bring food and medicines.

He had much to attend to that morning. The disorganized poor box needed sorting if he was to bring what the farmers needed. Unbidden, he reflected that Sally's sure hands had always taken care of that task for him. Like her biscuits at the morning table, he missed her industry. He relived how she had turned away from him at the dance. He would need to muddle through preparations without her aid.

"Must you? I need my horse this afternoon. Could not your love life wait one day?"

Frederick inhaled and let the air out at a measured pace. "I've been thinking about that. What if I bought a horse of my own? There is space in the shed for a second beast." He said without missing a beat, "I do have prize money. I'll purchase extra hay and grain so it will not be a burden to the church."

Edward felt like arguing about the expense, but

then considered that he would be able to do his work unimpeded. "What will become of your mount once you return to the sea?"

"I'll sell it. Would this not be the reasonable course? Each of us could sail to our own destinations unimpeded."

Before Edward could respond, Mrs. Bates entered the kitchen. She pulled a pair of envelopes from her apron. "These arrived for you both." She handed a slim envelope to Edward and a larger packet to his brother.

Edward opened the envelope at the table, foregoing a trip to his study for privacy. The envelope contained an invitation to a supper dance at the Bowers for both himself and Frederick. "We are invited to the Bower's event next Friday night." Edward's voice was neutral. He felt tired by the idea of women ignoring him and having to go through the formalities of dancing. Have they not attended enough parties for one season?

His brother set the packet unopened in front of his plate. He stirred his eggs with a fork, but did not eat. "Frederick?"

His brother's attention snapped to him, the somber expression quirked into his usual casual grin. "We are expected." Frederick raised an eyebrow at him. "I understand that Miss Sally will be attending."

"Why should that have any bearing if we go or not?" Edward said.

"Why indeed?" Frederick's grin grew broader.

Edward scowled. "Are you not going to open your packet?" Frederick's jovial mood vanished. He looked at the package of oilcloth, the sort of weather proof encasement the navy used to send missives to its officers.

"Aye. I should." Frederick used his clasp knife and cut the twine around the oilcloth. There were many folded sheets enclosed, embossed with a red wax seal. His brother read the contents of the missive and then set it down. His express was stricken.

"What is wrong? Are you well?"

Frederick nodded and swallowed. When he spoke it was with a steady voice, but devoid of emotion. "I am offered a ship. The Asp is an old frigate. She has seen better days, but with the right crew, she will be ready to answer the call of duty." He said with an absent air, "I should send for Harville to be my first lieutenant."

Edward felt a surge of disappointment, for a ship meant that Frederick would be leaving Monkford. For all the man irritated him, he was his brother. With the Napoleonic war waging, there would be no knowing when he would ever see Frederick again. "When do you take possession?"

"In a fortnight."

"Is this not what you have hoped for?"

"Aye, it 'tis. Promotion to Captain and a ship of my own is all I dreamed of since the day I joined the navy." Frederick shrugged, "But this does not leave much time."

"Time for what?"

Frederick gave him a helpless look. "For Anne. I had hoped for more time to court the girl, but it seems the navy is forcing me to declare myself prematurely."

Edward remembered Lady Russell's previous threats. While he thought that the girl would be easy enough for his brother to win over, the family would be less forgiving. "The Elliots are highly placed in the community. They may not view you as worthy of a baronet's daughter."

His brother shot him a glare. "If what I am and what I will become is not enough, it is on them, not I."

Edward held up his palm to indicate that he understood and the glare receded. "You will have to act fast if you mean to secure her."

"Miss Anne is everything I could want in a wife; beautiful, amiable, and educated. If I don't act now, before I return from the sea, she will marry some lordling with bad breath and poorer manners."

Edward recalled Lady Russell's idea for her god-daughter to marry a man of wealth and title. His brother was not far from the mark. "What is your plan?"

"I am going to offer for her at the Bower's supper dance. It will give me time afterward to approach her father and gain his consent before I ship out." Frederick displayed all the confidence of a captain going into battle. Defeat was not an option.

"There will be no time to read the banns before you depart." Over the course of three Sundays, the banns proclaimed a couple's intent to marry in the church of their families. It allowed all to know of the happy news before the event and for anyone who objected to have time to make their displeasure known.

"I will go to London and obtain a special license. Then, if you will indulge me, you could perform the ceremony for us?"

A special license was expensive, but it would solve the time problem. His brother could marry and still claim his ship on schedule. This was fast work indeed. Edward stood from the table. "I would be honored, but perhaps we should wait before planning the wedding breakfast. The lady needs to say yes first."

###

Frederick wore his new navy blue frock coat with a gold watch fob tucked into his vest. He wore a stylish top hat and leather gloves of the finest kidskin. Frederick spared no expense on his wardrobe for the Bower's supper dance. He had paid the tailor an extra fee to make sure his garments were ready in time for this event. He had insisted on riding his new horse, a coal black stallion with a temper.

Edward drove beside him, seated in his cart with

the faithful gelding trotting down the country road. He wore the same coat he always did, but he had taken extra effort to be presentable. When the Bower grooms came to take their horses, Edward noticed that Frederick's horse gained looks of appreciation from the men. Edward hopped from the cart and waited by the gelding's head until a groom came for the patient beast. "Let me take the old boy, Mr. Wentworth." Edward released the horse and joined his brother who was hitting his gloves in one hand as he stared at the entrance of the Bower residence.

"Are you ready?" Edward said. Frederick startled at the sound of his voice. He gave a curt nod and the pair stepped onto the path that led to the door. At the entrance, Mr. And Mrs. Bower greeted their guests as they streamed in from the various carriages, carts and contrivances of the county. When their turn arrived, Edward gave a polite bow to his hosts.

"Mr. Wentworth, how good of you to come. I trust that you are well?" The matron returned his bow with a smooth, well-practiced curtsy.

"Indeed, Mrs. Bower. Let me say that it does my soul good to see you up and about."

The matron waved a hand at the curate. "Oh tosh, how could I not recover with such boon companions to attend me?" She smiled at Edward's brother, "Is that not true, Commander?"

Frederick took the woman's hand into his own and bowed over it. "I thank you for your kind invitation to visit these past few weeks. It has made my shore leave more pleasant than any sailor has a right to expect." Mr. and Mrs. Bowers exchanged an amused glance as Edward and his brother gave their leave.

The sounds of violin strings and the tickle of a piano warned Edward that the first dances were to begin. Frederick was glowering toward the front door. He leaned over to Frederick. "Patience. I'm sure she will be here soon."

Frederick let out his breath at a measured rate. "Aye. I know the Elliots will come. As usual, Sir Walter is fashionably late."

Edward gave an absent nod in response, but his attention wandered to the other side of the room. Seated upon a settee, Sally Marshall appeared radiant in the sunbeams from a nearby window. There were golden highlights in her hair and the light spilled over her peach and white muslin dress. From her wrist dangled a tiny book. She was talking to three young men who seemed to captivated for his comfort. When one of them signed her book, Edward felt the air leave his lungs in a forceful manner.

This time, Frederick leaned toward him. "Victory goes to the bold, Edward. Hesitation can lose the battle."

"I find that some hesitation can be beneficial, Brother. If I make a misstep, there could be repercussions."

"How can there be repercussions for talking to a girl at a party?"

Was he being too cautious? Frederick was planning on offering to the lady he chose, no matter her status or the outcome. Nothing would stand in the way of what he wanted. Edward was not sure if Sally would give him notice, but until he tried, he would not know for sure.

At the entrance, a loud voice announced. "Sir Walter Elliot. Lady Russell. Miss Elliot. Miss Anne Elliot."

Frederick inhaled a long breath and pulled himself to his full height. This was the moment his brother waited for. "Wish me luck, Brother."

"Go with God." Edward watched his brother stride across the room toward his Anne. The girl had eyes for no one but Frederick, transformed by the emotions within, her happiness radiant upon her face for all to see. Frederick gave his lady a bow and waited for her corresponding curtsy before taking her hand. Within moments, the pair had separated from Anne's party. His brother was far too occupied to notice what Edward did, Lady Russell glaring at the sailor. She tapped her fan on Sir Walter's arm to point the pair out, but the baronet was too busy with a group of men that had come to him for conversation.

When music began, the dancers formed lines and began the intricate steps of the dance, weaving back and forth between the facing rows. Edward studied the pairs until he spotted Sally with her first partner. He took a spot along the wall until one of his parishioners approached. Soon he became locked in a discussion about the man's plantings and family. The curate was not able to get away during the pause in the music, without insulting the man he was conversing with. He noticed that once more Sally was off with a new partner. He had hesitated and thus others had filled the girl's dance card.

At last the parishioner departed and Edward had a moment to himself. He poured a cup of punch and lifted it to his lips. It would not be long before the supper dance and then the meal. No doubt, the Bowers would expect him to give grace since the Vicar was absent.

There was a swish of fabric behind him. Stunned, Edward turned to face a blushing Sally Marshall. Edward gave her a bow and the girl curtsied. "Good evening, Miss Marshall. What brings you here?"

A frown creased her fair face. "It is your brother. He is not keeping to two dances with Miss Anne as is proper. Can you speak to him before more people talk?"

She was about to say more, but with a flush of jealous ire, Edward cut her off. "Why? So that you may claim him before it is too late?"

Sally took an involuntary step back. "Mr. Wentworth, it is not that. I overheard…."

The ire turned to exasperation. "After all this time, you could use my Christian name. Must we be so formal or is that you prefer it that way?"

"No." Sally straightened and touched her hair. "I never preferred that, but you are the curate of this parish and never invited me to speak otherwise."

Edward deflated, seeing the hurt brewing in her fine eyes. What had his brother said about hesitation? "If I invited you now?" He could not breathe as he awaited her answer.

"I would like that, Edward."

The musicians were preparing for the next dance and Edward speculated which of the young men would be claiming Sally this time. He breathed deep to steady his nerves. "If you are not claimed for this dance, would you do me the honor of standing up with me?" He crooked his arm and held it out.

Sally stepped closer to him and tucked her hand under his forearm. "Nothing would please me more." He felt a rush of heat to his collar as he led them out to the dance floor.

As Edward began the steps to the reel with Sally who stood in the line across from him, he noted the smile on her face and the way she met his gaze. There was no coyness from her tonight. How could he have been that blind in thinking of her as a child? There was nothing about her now that would indicate this. He took in her slim waist and the slender ankles that peeked out from under her skirt as she moved. Sally Marshall was now a grown woman.

When the music ended, Edward led Sally outside onto the terrace, the cool night air welcome after their exertions. The moonlight made Sally glow like an angel, he wanted to stroke the blonde tresses of her hair and caress her cheek. Such actions would be improper and he would not dishonor her. The pair leaned on the railing.

"You are beautiful tonight, Sally." He relished using her Christian name.

"It is good of you to notice." She paused. "At last."

Edward felt surprise. "Have I been as dense as my brother suggested?"

She studied his face. "I had given up hope that

you would see me. Even my coming out this spring did not seem to reach you." She shook her head as if at a naughty child. "You can be rather focused on your work, Edward."

Edward stroked his chin. He reminisced about all the time they spent together. He had always spoken about his work to her, but seldom asked about herself as a person. As a curate, the well-being of everyone in his parish should be paramount to him and yet he had neglected Sally's feelings. "I have been remiss with you, Sally. Can you accept my apology?"

Sally smiled at him. "It is already forgotten, Edward."

Edward had seen all the men dangling after her. What had changed tonight? He reached over and took her hand and felt a jolt go through him as she allowed the familiarity. "I am glad of that, but I find that I'm confused. I'm just a curate without much to offer as compared to the other men seeking your favor."

"You have more to offer than most men, Edward Wentworth." Sally squeezed his hand. "I have never met a man as kind and thoughtful as you. Many curates would do the work for their Vicar as a mere profession, but you have honest feelings for those that you tend. I find that quite admirable." Her blue eyes gazed into his with an intensity that negated the cool evening breeze.

Edward felt his face grow warm at her praise. He knew he should not, but he leaned over and kissed her. She tasted sweet like honey and lavender. He felt her arms slip around his waist as she kissed him in return. When they came up for air, Edward and Sally pressed their foreheads together, each not letting the other go.

"Will you join me for the supper dance?" His voice was a whisper.

"I will." She touched the side of his face and he closed his eyes, not daring to breath. Sally departed for the ballroom and he watched her go with a pounding heart, but extreme happiness.

Edward turned back to the darkness of the garden, willing his heart to slow down. To his surprise, he detected movement in the moonlight. A couple was walking side by side on the garden path. Edward realized that it was his brother and Anne Elliot. The couple stopped and his brother knelt on one knee. He held his love's hand and looked up at her as he spoke. At the girl's enthusiastic nod, Frederick stood and took the girl into his arms, whirling her around him in joy. The boldness of his brother had produced his desired result this evening. Edward turned away, giving the couple their privacy.

The door to the ballroom opened behind him. Edward expected that his Sally had returned.

Instead the sight of a bobbing ostrich feather greeted him. Lady Russell marched onto the terrace, a frown marring her expression. Edward considered his brother out in the garden with Anne.

Stepping away from the railing, Edward moved to meet the matron near the door, where she could not see out into the darkness.

"Lady Russell. What a surprise. Can I be of service to you?"

"Mr. Wentworth, I am seeking your brother. Where is he?"

"I am not certain."

The woman pursed her lips. "Perhaps you are the brother I should speak to." The matron gave Edward an expectant look. "It has come to my attention that my god-daughter has not been alone at this residence. I have it on good report that your brother has been visiting the Bowers on a regular basis. It is during the same time that my Anne has been here keeping Mrs. Bower occupied. I must know what his intentions toward my god-daughter are."

Edward thought of the scene he had just witnessed. He knew his brother's plans, but it was not his place to speak of them. Frederick had not broken with the girl's father yet. "I cannot speak for my brother's intentions, but I suspect that he does care for Miss Anne."

"He is a sailor and we all know what sort of men those are!"

"He is an officer of his majesty's navy, a man that protects England from invasion by putting his own life in peril."

"My husband died on the peninsula due to the navy not arriving to save his regiment. I will never trust a naval officer again. My Anne can do much better." She peered up at him, using her glasses. "You would do well to remember that your living and home is on the suffrage of Sir Walter Elliot, the most predominate man in this county. Should the baronet learn of your brother's transgressions, it will not go easy for you."

Edward felt a chill go down his spine. His ability to court Sally would be over if he lost his position. Without a reference from his Vicar, he would not find another job and find himself penniless on the road. Still, he had to defend his brother. It was a matter of family honor. "If Anne cares for him, why are you so against this union? Do you not care for her happiness?"

"Anne is nineteen years old. She is young and full of prospects. Why should she throw her life away on a sailor that could go to the bottom of the ocean at any time? She could have a learned man who might remain home to protect and provide for her and her future children. Perhaps even a man with a title and an estate."

"While my brother has little to recommend but himself now, I assure you he is rising in the ranks of the navy. His feelings are genuine for Anne. This must count for something even in your circle."

Lady Russell stood up. "I see that speaking to you is useless. I will appeal directly to my god-daughter and will make her see reason!"

The matron whirled and re-entered the party. Edward glanced back at the garden behind him. His brother and Anne were still out there in the moonlight, locked in each other's arms, oblivious to the world around them.

###

Edward had called upon Sally late that morning, as he had done twice a week since the Bower's Supper Dance a fortnight ago. Sally's mother would serve tea and her younger sister would join the family as they chatted about the people of the parish. It was rare for Mr. Marshall to join them, but he had come home early from the apothecary shop in the village. He handed Edward a small basket of phials.

"This is for Mother Higgins. You will let us

know how she fares?"

"Of course."

Mr. Marshall glanced at Sally who was putting on her pelisse and bonnet. The new custom was for Sally to walk with him to the cottage, chaperoned by her younger sister. It allowed Edward to obtain the medicines he used in his ministry and gave him an excuse to call on her. "I suspect we'll see you again at the usual appointed hour?" Sally's father delivered with a touch of merriment.

"I assure you, Sir, I will." Sally joined him at the door with her sister not far behind. Edward gave his farewell to Sally's parents and the three young people began their trek down the country lane. Sarah walked with them in the beginning, taking in the russet hued trees and green fields with delight. As time passed, the girl slowed her steps until she followed at a respectful distance behind them. Sarah would not allow the couple out of her sight, but they could converse with some privacy.

"Has your brother returned from his journey? You mentioned he was off to London."

"He returned yesterday."

"Since he came here to Monkford, you have changed. You will miss his counsel, once he returns to the sea." Although his brother's rag manners had upset the order in his life, he had come to realize that some of his brother's boldness had rubbed off on him.

Sally took his gloved hand into her own. "It was your brother that told me to not give up hope and to try a different tack with you. I thought him mad at first, but in the end, he was right. My idea of making you jealous drove you away instead of bringing you closer."

Edward chuckled and tightened his grasp on her

hand. "There is no danger of you driving me away any longer, my dear." He shook his head at the irony of his next statement. "Frederick took my advice and is off to Kellynch Hall to speak with Sir Walter Elliot. He will ask for Anne's hand this afternoon." His brother showed him the special marriage license he had purchased in London. It cost most of his prize money, but the result elated Frederick.

"Everyone could see how taken they were of each other at the dance a fortnight ago. I realize that many feel your brother is aiming too high with his suit, but I think Anne is a lucky girl."

"As do I. She seems a sweet and amiable girl. I think she will make my brother happy." He held up a hand of caution. "Not a word of this to anyone, Sally. I promised Frederick that this news would remain within family."

"Am I now considered family?" There was a

teasing tone to the girl's voice.

Edward halted and studied her pretty face. He had spoken nothing formal to her about their understanding and his hope for their future together. He enjoyed taking the time to know the young woman behind the frilly curls and winsome smile that courtship allowed. Yet, marriage was a growing subject in his mind and one that he realized that he relished.

"I believe you are fishing for compliments, my dear." Sally seemed amused by his response. Perhaps she too realized that time was on friendly terms with their relationship. There was no need to hurry. The pair resumed their walk toward his cottage.

All too soon the three reached the garden gate of his cottage. Sally's sister remained many paces away, within sight, but out of hearing.

"We part company once more, Sir." Sally said.

He did not release her hand. "I wish I could invite you in for tea, but your poor sister has been accommodating enough this morning."

"One day I will be able to stay, but until then…" she squeezed his hand. Edward felt a need to kiss her upturned face, but that would not be proper. He intended to back away, but Sally moved closer and suddenly he did not care what was proper. He leaned over and touched her lips with his own and heard a soft sigh from the girl as they parted. They held hands a moment more and then Sally stepped back and joined her sister. The two girls departed on the road, leaning to gossip together with each turning to look back at him at various points on the road. Their merriment made Edward smile. Once they were out of sight, he opened the gate and walked through the garden. The young curate entered the cottage via the side door.

Inside, Mrs. Bates was kneading bread. She gave her employer a worried look as he entered. "Mr. Wentworth, the Vicar is here to see you. I let him into your study." Edward set the basket of medicines on the kitchen table. "He has not been here long. Perhaps a half hour."

The Vicar sat in a wingback chair near the fire in the study. He had a cup of tea on the table beside him and was reading one of Edward's books. When Edward came into view, the Vicar closed the book and gave his curate a measured stare. "Good day, Edward. Were you off visiting the Marshalls again?"

Edward paled. How much the Vicar had heard of his courting and did he approve? "Yes, Sir."

The Vicar waved his hand. "I am not here to lecture about your personal life. If you wish to pay court to a woman, that is your concern, not mine. However, another matter has come to my attention."

The Vicar indicated that Edward should take the other chair. The young curate sat and waited for his employer to speak.

"Lady Russell came to visit me a few days ago. She is most displeased about your brother's conduct with her god-daughter. She said that she spoke to you about the matter, but her words fell on deaf ears."

"She did speak to me, Father, but I did not feel that it was my place to act."

"Go on."

"She expressed concern about my brother's attentions toward Anne Elliot. I felt that it was Miss Elliot's father's duty to protect the girl, not Lady Russell's. Anne's father did not seem concerned. When Lady Russell mentioned that the navy had failed to protect her husband's regiment, I felt her bias toward all members of the Royal Navy, including my brother."

"What are your brother's intentions toward the girl?"

"Completely honorable. He has gone this afternoon to break with Anne's father and ask his permission to marry her."

"That is well, considering the girl is under the age of consent. I am glad to learn that he does not plan to elope with her." The Vicar nodded to himself. "How much longer will your brother be here in Monkford?"

"He will be departing soon, sir. He has a commission to captain a new ship."

"I hesitate to enter into a situation between a father and his daughters. It is not as if Miss Anne is an orphan, however Lady Russell feels."

"That was my thought as well."

The Vicar remained quiet as he looked into the fire. When he spoke, he did not look at Edward. "Lady Russell has demanded that I release you from my service. She is a large benefactor to the church and has threatened to cut off her tithe if I do not give in to her wishes."

Edward felt the heat of anger, but was careful to keep it from his face. "I see. I will pack my belongings and leave when you wish. I would request that you give time to allow Mrs. Bates to arrange for lodging with her family."

The Vicar turned to his curate. "Edward, do not be ridiculous. You have been one of the better curates I have hired in years. I will not turn you out without a reference. While I respect Lady Russell, who works in my parish is my own decision."

The tension within Edward subsided.

"The lady is not without heart, lad. She is wrong to threaten you and your brother, but she does so out of love for her god-daughter. She wants what is best for Anne." He gave Edward a stern look. "Her point about how the Commander could die in battle and leave Anne penniless is not unheard of. It happens all to often during wartime. Your family has no connections and no wealth. Who would take care of the girl if she married your brother and the worse happened?"

"She would have a home with me, as my sister. That is, if her own family did not wish to care for her. Was this Lady Russell's sole objection?"

"There were several others. The woman can be quite persuasive."

"What do you propose to do?" Edward said.

"I know of two openings. One is a curate

position to the north. It would pay about the same as I afford you here, but it would remove you from Lady Russell's wrath. I bring it up as an option of last resort. The other is a rectory in Shopshire. I have thought to write to the retiring rector and give my personal recommendation for you to become his replacement. With god's grace, he will accept you."

A living offered to him? With that he could make Sally an offer of marriage and have everything he wanted; a position of respect as Rector and the money to support a wife and children. The main loss would be leaving Monkford and all the people he had been tending for the past two years, but for a promotion it would be worth the move.

"I am not sure what to say, Father. Thank you."

"With your brother leaving and if I can manage this promotion for you within a half year or so, this should appease Lady Russell. She need not know that you move on to a better life. I had heard of you courting the Marshall girl, I was hesitant to offer this idea since I feared you would not want to leave our parish due to her."

"Miss Marshall will be pleased for me."

"Good." The Vicar stood and offered his hand to Edward. They shook on the bargain. "Go with God, Edward. I will see you next Sunday at service."

Edward sat in his study for a long time. The passage of time meant little. He poured himself a brandy and swirled the amber liquid in its glass. This was proving to be a day of momentous portents. He hoped that his brother was as fortunate in his own commission at Kellynch Hall.

###

In the early evening, there was a quiet rap on his study's door. "Enter," he bade, closing his book.

"Sir, it is young Daniel from the village. He wishes to speak to you." Mrs. Bates scowled, her heavy set face showing her displeasure, "It is about Commander Wentworth."

Young Daniel Collins was a likable urchin, who worked in the stables of the Cock and Crow, the pub in Monkford's village square. "I'll receive him here. If you would, Mrs. Bates."

As Edward set his book aside on the small table beside his overstuffed leather chair, the boy shuffled into the study. His ragged clothing and dirty hair looking out of place in the curate's tidy home. He wrung his cap in his hands.

"Ah, Master Collins. What brings you here?"

"If you please, Sir. Mr. Spencer sent me to find you. It is about your brother. Commander Wentworth." The boy kept his eyes on the russet carpet.

Edward sat up in his chair in alarm. "What has happened? Is my brother well?"

"Mr. Spencer said that you needed to come. He did not think that the Commander could sit a horse in his condition. Beggin' yer pardon, Sir."

"His condition?" The question was not posed to the boy, but rather to himself. The feeling of dread that had clung to him throughout the afternoon, when no word had come from his brother, intensified. He gave young Master Collins a nod. "Allow me to get my coat and we will attend to my brother straight away."

Edward hitched his gelding to the cart and soon he and the boy were on their way back to Monkford, pulling into the yard of the Cock and Crow Pub. As Edward tied the reins of the gelding to the horse bar, he could hear the loud, slurred words of a sea shanty coming from inside. He winced at the sound. His brother had a fine singing voice when he was sober. Judging from the slurred words and the flat key, Frederick was well into his cups. The curate turned to the boy, "Is my brother's horse in the stable?"

"Yes, Mr. Wentworth."

Edward dug out a coin and handed it to the boy. "Gather my brother's saddle and other gear and place it in the cart. Tie his horse to the back. I will not be long." Upon those words, Edward entered the establishment. When his eyes had adjusted to the dim light, Edward gave a nod to Mr. Spencer who stood behind the bar, white rag in his hand as he polished a glass. The man pointed toward a private palor to the rear. It was still early and there were a mere handful of patrons in the pub. The farmers and sheep herders drank their brew. A barmaid circulated among them, bringing more drink as needed. There was no broken furniture, which relieved the curate. Edward found his brother at a table, a tankard of ale in his hand, used to gesture as he sang. It sloshed over the arm of his brother's best dress uniform, soaking into the dark blue material.

"Ho Edward!" cried out his brother as Edward approached. "Come and join me for a round."

"Frederick?" He kept his arms from the wooden

surface, for it was wet with spilled ale. "Are you well?"

"Why would I not be?" Frederick took another swig of the amber brew, "Are not all sailors blessed with my sort of luck?"

"I take it that your meeting with Sir Walter did not go well." The curate lowered his voice, hoping that his brother would follow his lead and do the same.

"That pompous jackass." He poked at his brother's chest with his finger, almost missing him due to poor aim. "You have no connections, no money and thus are a nobody," Frederick mimicked Sir Walter's tenor voice and upper class accent before he slammed his hand on the table. "The navy awarded me an a commendation at San Domingo for my quick thinking and action, but to Anne's father, I'm a nobody!"

"Sir Walter refused to give you permission to marry Anne?" Edward had suspected as much from the baronet. Sir Walter was a proud man. Although Anne was not his favorite daughter, he would still have standards about who he would allow her to marry.

"No." Frederick shook his head and the action caused him to grip the table to steady himself. "He gave his consent, but in the most degrading of manner. He told me that he would cut Anne off from her rightful inheritance and that there would be no dowry. He thought that would turn me away." The sailor looked deep into his cup. "In his world, money and connections are the sole reason to marry. What one feels is secondary."

Edward felt confused. "So you decided to not marry Anne due to her lack of dowry? I thought you loved her."

Frederick slammed the table again, causing the

wooden table to teeter. Edward jumped back from the sharp sound. "I do...did love her," bitterness tinged Frederick's voice. "I found Anne in the library soon after speaking to her father. I told her what he had said and that it did not matter. I wanted her for herself and no other reason. The lack of a dowry would not change my offer."

"I'm pleased to hear that."

Frederick looked off into the air, as if seeing the woman before him. "She looked as if she had been crying, but before I could ask her why, she broadsided me that she had changed her mind. She said that for my own good, she would not marry me." His voice became a whisper. "She said that if I married her, I would not take the risks necessary to further my career. The woman I love rejected me, set me adrift without so much as consulting my wishes in the matter, because of my boldness."

"Frederick, she is nineteen and you have been

pushing her toward marriage with undue speed. Perhaps she needs more time."

The Commander turned away and looked at the wall in silence. He set his tankard on the table. "She is too timid be a sailor's wife. She thought the life too hard or perhaps that I would not be constant to her. Whatever the reason, I am done. I have no wish to continue my suit. Indeed, I would leave this place. Return to what I know and understand."

Edward felt his heart lurch. "You will be leaving my company as well. I have enjoyed having you here this past summer."

Guilt crossed the young commander's face. "I will miss you too, but every moment I remain here is agony." Frederick lifted his mug peering into the depths of the cup. "I thought that drink might dull the pain, but all it creates is melancholy."

"And will give you a monster of a headache in

the morning, to be certain." Edward offered Frederick his hand. "Come. Let us go home. Maybe in the morning things will seem clearer after a good night's sleep?"

Frederick grasped Edward's hand and allowed his brother to pull him to his feet. The sailor was unsteady and his brother put an arm around his shoulder to help guide him toward the door.

###

Edward finished hitching the gelding to the cart and stood holding the animal's bridle. His brother's stallion remained in the shed. His brother charged Edward to sell the beast later and donate the money to the church.

Frederick strode out the front door, dressed in his blue and gold naval uniform. A bicorn adorned his head at a slight angle and the buttons of his jacket gleamed. The sailor heaved his seachest to the back of the cart and secured it with a rope. As the two brothers climbed into the cart, Edward could still smell the ale on his brother's breath.

"Mrs. Bates prepared a strong tea this morning. I trust you availed yourself of it."

"My compliments to the esteemed Mrs. Bates." Frederick's voice was flat and lifeless. Edward slapped the reins across the gelding's rump and the horse broke into an easy trot. The post would stop in Monkford within the hour, and his brother would be on it.

"Are you sure you wish to leave? Perhaps you could salvage the situation with Anne with time."

"My ship awaits, Edward. I must report to Plymouth for my duty. My error was to allow my heart to stray from the sea. I will not make that mistake again."

Edward considered the new understanding

between himself and Sally, an understanding that brought him pleasure, but a sense of completeness. He wished the same outcome for his seafaring brother. "If you cannot stay, would you consider writing to Anne? In time, she might regret her choice."

Frederick frowned. "I doubt that any letter of mine would reach her. That harpy god-mother would see to it. No. It is over and I am well rid of her. I want a woman who knows her own mind, who I can trust to be waiting for me when I return to England."

They entered the yard of the humble inn where the post chaise would stop. Edward tied the gelding to one of the rail posts and stood beside the cart. His brother lifted his seachest and set it onto the dusty road. The post chaise pulled into the yard. A carter from the post lifted the sailor's seachest to the baggage rack. His brother stood near the driver's seat, intending to ride in the open air. Edward embraced his brother in farewell. He felt gratified when his brother reciprocated. "My thanks for putting me up during shore leave, Edward."

"It was my pleasure. The next time you are in England, know that you will be welcome."

Frederick appraised him with a measured stare and then a nod. "You are the better brother, Edward. I thought you a prissy bluestocking when I first arrived, but now I see your inner strength. I do not have the patience you do. I am more suited to the harshness of the sea." He turned and looked down the road. "It will be good to claim my ship and set sail again."

Frederick climbed aboard the post and settled into the seat beside the driver, the gold bullion of his uniform catching the sunlight. Edward stepped away and watched the post depart Monkford, taking his brother home to the sea.

THE END

Thank you for reading
The Curate's Brother

If you liked the book, please consider leaving a positive review on Amazon. It is of great help to any independent author and I'd love to hear from you.

BIOGRAPHY

Wendy Van Camp makes her home in Southern California with her husband. She enjoys travel, camping, bicycling, gourmet cooking and gemology.

Wendy has published two short memoirs in "Shadows Express Magazine", Scifaiku Poetry in "Quantum Visions" and "Far Horizons" Magazines and one regency romance on Amazon.

"The Curate's Brother" is the first story of a series featuring the characters of Jane Austen's novel "Persuasion".

NO WASTED INK:

Wendy Van Camp's writing blog features
articles about the craft of writing, interviews of
science fiction and fantasy authors, book reviews of
classic science fiction and fantasy novels, a weekly
writer's link roundup and general announcements
about the various short stories, poetry and novels
that I am currently publishing.

Come and visit:
http://nowastedink.com

LINKS

Website: No Wasted Ink

http://nowastedink.com

Twitter: wvancamp

https://www.twitter.com/wvancamp

Facebook: No Wasted Ink

http://www.facebook.com/nowastedink

No Wasted Ink Newsletter: Sign Up Today

http://eepurl.com/2EfpH

The newsletter is quarterly and is for announcements of new releases by the author.

21703149R00070

Printed in Great Britain
by Amazon